Author:

Bry Johnson.

Title:

My Football Boots don't fit.

Use Flip-flops Mr England.

Chapter 1

There once lived three little boys called Mr. Lion, Mr. Nuts and Mr. Little.

Mr. Lion's ambition was to score lots of goals for ENGLAND, but each time he tried to kick a football he hit a rock. Despite this, he was confident he will win the match.

Mr. Nuts told his parents, at quite a young age, that he wanted to play for ENGLAND when he grew up, but he was fat and ugly.

His friends called him a "monster nut" because his face resembled one.

Whilst, Mr. Little wasn't peculiar about his choices. They lived in a tiny little village called Wallington. It was winter and full dark had fallen.

In Wallington, they deserted the streets in winter before 10pm, only the foxes dared brave the cold winter nights.

I can understand; it's because they were homeless.

Mr. Lion asked, "Why are most boy's wilder than girls?"

"That's because they are meant to be kept in a pen," laughed Mr. Nuts.

"Well, I can say its wild nuts," added Mr. Lion alarmingly.

"Why are nuts wild?" demanded Mr. Little.

Mr. Lion replied, "it's because they have no owners."

"I wonder why Mr. Nuts isn't in a shell?" declared Mr. Lion.

"Perhaps he just escaped his prison!" answered Mr. Little.

"Why do you mistake me for a nut?" puzzled Mr. Nuts.

"A moment ago you claimed that I am a fruit nut, and now you are saying I am nuts.

Mr. Nuts knew he was ugly, but his actions didn't resemble a monster by any account. However, he was mischievous and provocative, but he hated been called a monster boy.

"I don't recognise the name monster as a description of myself," announced Mr. Nuts.

Mr. Little replied, "Who are you then?"

He suggested, "he may be nuts but not a monster or a fruit nut."

"If I give you a mirror, you will run away from yourself." asserted Mr. Little aloofly.

"I am an aspiring footballer," when have you heard a footballer being called a freak?

"Except biting Suarez" replied Mr. Little.

"You aren't Suarez," declared Mr. Lion.

"Mr. Nuts it's just a joke. You deserve to be feared on the pitch, that commands respect. That's why we call you "monster" because your opponents refuse to tackle you on the pitch. Managers know their players are too frightened to carry out their instructions to tight mark you."

He laughed.

"I thought it meant us to eat Mr. Nuts roasted, dry or raw tomorrow," repeated Mr. Lion.

"Please don't tell him, it's supposed to be top secret." declared Mr. Little.

Mr. Nuts responded, "don't be silly."

Mr. Lion replied, "if I have any of that nut I will go nuts,"

"Isn't Mr. Nuts crazy, why are you trying to compare him with wild nuts?" asked the referee.

Mr. Lion suggested "when Mr. Nuts cries the pitch is too big." That's because you are losing, isn't it?

The Coach told him when he grew up he would fix his legs, weight, so he doesn't have to foul his opponents any more.

"How is this possible? Perhaps I am being mistaken for Pele by my Coach," wondered Mr. Nuts.

Those that have seen Mr. Nuts play football told me he just splatters himself at the experiences of the opposition players on the soccer pitch.

Perhaps he feared the opposition's faces as they resembled a drunk villain.

As for Mr. Lion, he was everywhere on the soccer pitch; it was like a tea plantation in the winter months.

Wallington was in the Surrey countryside. Its lush mellows blossom in the spring months, it was a green and pleasant place to live and work. Its fishponds were one draw for tourists in the village. It had a rich history of former and serving military personnel. On the high Street, there was a library and rolls of shops decorated by shop signs and street's lights.

Football was the past time for kids in the park and streets corners.

The coach of Mr. Lion, Mr. Nuts and Mr. Little was sceptical about their ability to climb to the top.

He told them he was the coach, and he had the vision not to pick them

They repeatedly asked 'Why?'

"I always tell them they are premature footballers," said the Coach.

Mr. Nuts replied, "if you don't choose me, Coach, I will give you rocks to scrub"

The Boys often enjoyed playing in the muck.

Someone has surprised me as their Coach when they told me 'it's because they were decent.'

Wallington had its city dwelling but also had remote fields and farm lands. Therefore, they could find mud to bath, perhaps they used being dirty despite the fortitude of being described as clean

I used to ask, 'Why is Mr. Nuts slow?' Was it perhaps because he was a Chameleon?'

Mr. Nuts suggested perhaps it was because he was big.

In fact, Nut's were made of lots of fat; if you chewed lots of them, they bound you to gain a mass of fat. However, Mr. Nuts was concerned about being entangled between the two names Nut and Nuts.

When I took a photo of Mr. Lion from the camera, the picture wasn't clear!

'I asked myself; is it because Mr. Lion was dirty?'

"No, it's the dirty opponents, I've just splattered mud on them, they better go home and have a bath," answered Mr. Lion.

Chapter 2

The players never complained about messy Mr. Little. They just accepted the fact that he was an amateur footballer, and all they wanted was to make Mr. Little run out of battery.

When the referee crashed into Mr. Lion.

I spoke to the fans, "Don't worry, it's not an accident, it's a foul."

As the game was going on, the referee ended the match.

When Mr. Lion asked 'Why?'

He replied, "it's because he was the goalkeeper."

The bouncer stopped the Coach from entering the pitch to ask the referee to continue the contest. When the Coach took him to court, he became like a baby in a cot.

The camcorder isn't working, but it had a picture of Mr. Lion one second ago.

"Was it in the same picture where the police camera caught the flu," inquired Mr. Lion.

"Perhaps it's because it went too long in the cold recording the race," said Mr. Nuts.

When the goalkeeper told me, he couldn't stop the football from entering the net, as their Coach I asked, "Why?"

He suggested that the event hadn't started yet, but Mr. Lion was already on the pitch playing soccer.

I quizzed frantically!

"Why did the goalkeeper allow the football into the net?"

I noticed it was because he had no hands!

Perhaps he had just had a fight? I suspect it was a boxing match.

The referee stopped the game because he thought the players had caught Coronavirus.

Actually, he was wrong because "it was the team bus that caught Coronavirus," Mr. Nuts denied.

We took the bus to the hospital, but there was no cure.

The goalkeeper used to allow lots of goals into the net because he was running after other players to wipe their boots.

"Send me a boot cleaner please, I need my toilet cleaned," said the ball boy.

'Why did a an ignorant man score?'

'It's because the goalkeeper didn't see the football.'

Even if the unconscious man had accepted a lens at all, the Ball boy would have removed the glasses.

The goalkeeper let the football into the net because the shot was too hot.

"Perhaps the football came from a nearby oven," said Mr. Lion with flushed cheeks.

"The referee sound his whistle to end the match at kick off?'

'It's because he forgot his legs' suggested Mr. Lion.

"I heard the referee was from Lego Land!" advised Mr. Lion.

Mr. Little replied, "let me play with the referee, perhaps he is a toy brick."

Toys from Lego Land were popular with young kids. They're the only way infants learn about the world. It gives them an insight into how things are done.

Mr. Little soon carried out his first brick home. I sought "if he had property insurance for his household?"

He replied, "no, but I have a certificate of warranty for all the materials used to construct the building." replied Mr. Lion.

"Why was the camera shooting blank?" questioned Mr. Lion.

Is the camera a gun?" inquired Mr. Nuts.

"I bought it from the Gunners," Mr. Nuts continued.

Mr. Nuts told the coach, as his jaw tightened, "Mr. Lion is tired. Can he retire?"

He acknowledged 'No!'

"He still has to play extra time! " Said the referee.

'Is the television recording the match?' demanded the Coach.

'No!'

"I just pressed the mute button on the camera!" said Mr. Nuts.

"The game has stopped, perhaps the referee is a toy?" Mr. Nuts suggested.

"I told him the Game has stopped because I have just stolen the referee's whistle." said Mr. Lion.

He asked, "Why is Mr. Nuts running up and down the football pitch? Is he training for the London marathon?"

In fact, it surprised me to see him on the starting blocks the following morning because he was a lazy athlete. His friends called him "The Naughty Todd" because he sounded like one. He slept the whole day and did very limited. He enjoyed playing in the mud. Perhaps that's why he announced himself an aspiring footballer?

"I think the match has just stopped, is Mr. Nuts tired?" asked Mr. Little

'No!'

"It's the football that is tired," said Mr. Little.

Is it a joke? Look at Mr. Nuts, puffing and sweating like a frog. I suggest you get him off the football pitch before he goes down like a fruit. If I were you, I would have him off and put him some drink of alcohol.

The Coach replied, "what if I get him soda, and he sinks to the ground?"

"He will drop anyway! The soda liquor is to relieve his suffering; if you send him to the bench right now, he will request soda juice to improve his taste." Mr. Lion suggested.

"When will the players leave the point for a break?" asked the football Coach.

'Next year!' said the referee.

"Referee, you are wicked! How can you expect my players to be running up and down the football pitch for a year?" asked the Coach.

"I am with them! Why the rush to go home? Is it because you are losing?" if you aren't careful I will add six-zero to the score line." threatened the referee.

The referee complained the players were uncertain.

The coach replied, "it's the rough football."

"A moment ago I was complaining my players need a break, and now you're telling me they are rough why won't you do the same!" said the Coach.

The captain has landed. Please record it shitting on the referee, Mr. Nuts suggested.

"Who is the owner of this eagle, like get it off my back!" the referee complained.

"Did you see that?" Mr. Nuts asked.

'What?' Mr. Lion responded.

"The referee fell to the ground" replied Mr. Little with his brain held backward.

'I heard the video recorder was damaged!'

'Wrong!'

'It's the television man.'

The referee complained I didn't record his burst trouser.

"Oh, the referee's brain is burst," added Mr. Nuts.

"Is that wine coming out of his head?" suggested Mr. Little.

"No! It's water" declared Mr. Nuts.

'Let me go a drink some water the tap has just opened.'

"Why is the referee crying?" asked Mr. Little.

"Maybe he has just been invited to the spice world tour, read Mr. Nuts.

'The record button is ruined!'

"No, it's the referee's legs that are separated" asserted Mr. Nuts.

"The referee is a toy brick from Lego Land," asserted Mr. Lion.

That's why he can't run.

"I wonder if I can use the referee's Lego toy bricks to build a sand castle?" spoke Mr. Lion

'Surprise he's only got a stone head?'

"Well, I am Keen to find out more about him," replied Mr. Lion.

"Is the camera recording?" asked Mr. Little.

'Yes!'

"Why there isn't a tape?" inquired Mr. Lion.

"Why is the referee slow?" asked Mr. Nuts with frowning, gritted teeth.

"He must have eaten coleslaw and some wheat, said Mr. Lion.

The referee was a sophisticated young college graduate, they fit him a healthy, perhaps it's the reason he had coleslaw and grain to increase his fat mass. He enjoyed all the unhealthy things that a footballer won't have to eat. I wonder if he gets into a fight with Mr. Nuts, who will win the battle.

"Is the referee crazy?" asked Mr. Nuts.

'Why?'

"He is running up and down the pitch," he continued.

The natural landforms in the suburb were wonderful. It was a suburb of forty-five houses, a Pub, Gym and a mini supermarket.

Mr. Nuts was determined to play the best football possible.

He suggested he could be better than Ronaldo.

"Why Ronaldo?" demanded Mr. Lion.

"Is Ronaldo good? Then he should do Charity work," said sarcastic Mr. Nuts.

Why do you salivate when Ronaldo dribbles football?

"It's because I admirer him and my saliva glans are full of joy," responded Mr. Little.

"Do you know how Football boots smell?" asked Mr. Lion.

'No!'

"It smells of poop because the players have shit on them," laughed Mr. Nuts.

Haven't they got manna's trying and out shout us? Perhaps there are crazy to even attempt to sing our songs.

It was no co incidents that football opponents enjoyed shouting and singing from the stands.

Chapter 3

"When I become a ENGLAND player, the screen will break each time I score a goal," continued Mr. Nuts.

"I believe that's why you are Nuts, how can a football net brake like a piece of fart?" demanded Mr. Lion with mouth hanged open.

"Have you seen a Boy play?" urged Mr. Little.

Mr. Lion replied, "no!"

"It's a fist fight!" he replied.

Mr. Lion was just six, the younger sibling of the three Boy's. Mr. Nuts was nine whilst Mr. Little was aged twelve.

"I am telling you I will be called the rocket man one day!" Mr. Nuts laughed.

'Are you an astronaut?'

"Where is the rocket head, is it a nuclear war head?" asked Mr. Lion.

"There is a fight in the ant colony, why not send a bomb there?" suggested Mr. Lion coolly.

"ENGLAND can soon count on my little Mini legs," Mr. Lion joked.

"Where are they?" claimed the Coach.

"Look at them, they stein like jellyfish," he replied.

"The opponent's smiles are fading," stated Mr. Little.

Mr. Little asked himself "why?"

"Is it because they are giving up?" quizzed Mr. Nuts.

"Now we can say the opponents are chickens," repeated Mr. Nuts.

"Is it because they are running away?" asked Mr. Lion.

'No! No!! It's the match that has faded.'

'Why?' Because the participants are rubbish.

"Perhaps the football is burst and falling air," suggested Mr. Little

'What's wrong with the football?'

"It must be a plane," added Mr. Nuts.

'No! The players are disappearing fast because they lack energy.'

'Why?' It's because they are electricians.

"Can't you see that they're an electric radiator because they generate heat," announced Mr. Nuts hollowly.

'The light is failing'

'Why?'

'It's because the goalkeeper has just gone blind.'

"When the referee's whistle fade's it means he is going for a shit," answered Mr. Lion.

"When I grow up, if I am not on the pitch, the referee won't start the game," said Mr. Lion.

"My name will be the Pele of England," did Mr. Nuts.

"Hah Pele come and clean my boots," asserted Mr. Lion.

"Rubbish" replied Mr. Little.

"Can a Baby kick football!" he asked.

"Don't be stupid, babies can only sleep a whole day," he added.

"Isn't it better than a football game?" said Mr. Nuts.

"Wait till I become a professional footballer I will let my opponents become babies," replied Mr. Lion.

The first time I stepped on to a pitch with the floodlights on, my emotions were wild. It felt as if I was in the jungle. As the fans sung unfamiliar tunes that were alien to me, I tried to joint in, but the words weren't familiar to me. My heart was racing with mixed feelings, I could have been a black racist. What if I don't fit into my new team, I may fit into a luncheon meat can? Am I good enough to kick an orange, now, but I will give it a go? How can I be the best? Perhaps it's by cheating.

Mr. Lion got himself a football club. His teammates couldn't understand why a Boy would want to play football. They concluded perhaps to breach them.

The league was in the lush suburbs of ENGLAND. The name of the club was ENGLAND LIONS. They played in the top tier of English soccer. The stadium was brilliant and everyone was welcoming, even though he was a Boy. His colleagues thought he was there to error and tackle their opponents. He replied, "I am here to play matches!"

Mr. Lion was signed at midnight on transfer deadline. The fans were excited about the news. His colleagues were pleased Jack Twitted can't wait to see you in the team bus. The next day at training he passed through the members only entrance the first time.

It was time for his original television interview.

The journalist asked him "why won't you play with your fellow Boy's,"

He replied, "I already do, just seeking new opportunities to fart more."

"Are you serious, you are treating the football pitch like a kindergarten, isn't it?" I suggest you better drink some baby milk, did the Coach.

As a player, they asked me "Are your football boots black?"

"Yes." he suggested.

"Then they must be racist against a black opponent," reported the referee.

"But boots don't fit, so I put on studs," Mr. Lion replied.

The audience laughed, and he laughed with them.

Then the Stewards asked Mr. Lion, are you the Coach?"

He replied, "No."

He spoke to Mr. Lion, "you are a space waster."

Mr. Lion replied, "don't worry, I will head home to see my babysitter."

"Is Ronaldo confused on the pitch?" asked the journalist.

'Yes!'

"That's because he saw me," responded Mr. Lion.

My understanding of football increased each time I stepped on the pitch.

'Who are you?'

'I am the magistrate! If perhaps you need a solicitor, I can be hired too.'

The very first time I tried to kick a ball, I missed it.

"Why!" Mr. Lion kicked an opponent.

"He snapped the opponents on his Bullock, he cried for a year without a reason. When the detective investigated the matter, they found that the football was poisoned," said the police.

Besides, he also noticed he can't head a Football.

"Why?" he is a stalk.

"The tail moved with him everywhere he passed, until the cat borrowed his hound and was never seen again," confessed Mr. Lion.

"Do you know the names of the fans?" demanded the journalist.

"No!" They are aliens. Mr. Lion replied.

"Yes, I can remember their names very well, I knew one of them as ET the alien," said Mr. Lion.

'Why are my football boots flat, ?' it's because they have got no feet in them.

"Is the ball foolish?" asked Mr. Nuts.

'Why?' it is heading in the contrary direction.

Mr. Lion told them he will be the player that opposite Fan's will hate to have one day.

When it happens, the opposite fans will be colour-blind, they won't be able to see Mr. Lion never again!" said Mr. Nuts.

'Why is the football white?' No idea.

"Could it be a Caucasian?" mocked Mr. Nuts.

Anyway, my eyes were on the football when I saw your girlfriend.

Chapter 4

I asked the referee "what size is the pitch?" he replied X Large.

'Where is the football?' the referee didn't let it on the pitch.

'Why!'

"It's because the football has caught Coronavirus," declared Mr. Nuts.

'Moreover, the football is flat, that's my house I better get in.'

"The football smells of poo," suggested Mr. Little.

'How comes!'

'The eagle has just pooped on it!'

"Where is the football?" asked Mr. Lion.

'Look at it racing.' is it a racist?'

'If you blow that soccer, I will punch your Bullock.' Mr. Lion, you are wicked.

'My name is Mr. Lion, my occupation is foot seller.'

"Mr. Lion, if you grow a tail on your brain you might lash the football" the press ridiculed him.

"Rubbish" he replied.

"Don't you know the prize of heading balls is air loss?" asked Mr. Lion.

"Wrong!" Why have I got facial hair?" demanded Mr. Nuts.

"Is your head Sponge?" because it absorbs the pain of every ball.

"If you run, you may fall, and I will laugh Ha-Ha-Ha," said the journalist

"Don't pretend to be a professional course you aren't," he ridiculed him.

"Is settling on the ground sweet because you laughed, how many sugars were in it?" demanded Mr. Lion.

The editor replied sarcastically, "nine that's my door number!"

"Are you a goalkeeper?" because you fell in love too fast, Mr. Lion " he ridiculously asked him.

"Go down to the grate is fun, each time you fall I laugh!" retorted the journalist.

"Mr. Lion don't turn around, you are racing a fart," he continued.

He joked, run faster, and you may catch the wind."

Someone from the crowd shouted at the referee, referee, referee, why are you raving?" he acknowledged the party isn't over yet.

"Coach, don't stand there and watch. Our opponents are fouling us," Mr. Nuts. Please come and play the rest of the match. We are tired.

"The league is jamming" are the players German?" asked Mr. Lion.

"Why are you jamming?" it's because the association has released me from prison, Mr. nuts suggested.

"Is this the pitch?" asked Mr. Lion.

"No, it's my spit" the Coach replied.

"The clay is dark." Is the soil African? Asked Mr. Lion questioned.

"No, it's from the sewer, did the referee.

"How dreadful is the pitch?" Mr. Little asked.

"It's as dangerous as a rotten egg," added the referee.

'Where are all my teammates?" asked Mr. Lion.

"They didn't let them in because the pitch is Covid-19 secure," the Coach replied.

"Is this the new turf?" Mr. Lion asked.

'Yes!'

"Why is it stretched up?" suggested Mr. Lion.

"The pitch is too big I can't run the length of it because I am patched up," repeated Mr. Lion.

"Is the pitch frozen?" asked the Coach.

"Yes!" Why didn't you get it out of the freezer, told Mr. Little?

'I need a forklift, '

"What for!" to get the pitch to my house, did Mr. Little.

'If the referee stumbled and fell, he would have to buy the pitch from the club,' he did.

'The referee is racing the length of the pitch!'

"Why?" urged Mr. Lion.

"He could be racist," stated Mr. Nuts.

"I demand to hire a shoplifter," suggested Mr. Lion.

"Why" pleaded Mr. Little.

"To take the frozen pitch out of the freezer," asserted Mr. Nuts.

"You spat at me!" Mr. Little shouted.

'Where is the spit?'

"Look at it running," asserted Mr. Little.

"My players are too big to fit through that door!" declared the Coach.

'Why is it?'

'Because they are obese.'

"What's the length of the match? "90 minutes, read the referee.

"How long can you go 45 seconds" too lazy, did the Coach alarmingly?

"Is the pitch frozen?" defrost it in a bake oven, expressed the Coach.

"How can you thaw a football in a bake oven like a pizza?" is the Coach mad, or perhaps he had eaten Mr. Nuts, suggested Mr. Lion.

"Green is my colour," added Mr. Nuts.

'Why?'

"Because I support Celtic," replied Mr. Nuts.

"Do you mean sell sticks?"

"No!"

"Celtic." Added Mr. Little.

"My foot is risen," announced Mr. Nuts.

"Can you manage it?" demanded the referee.

"When did I become a manager?" asked Mr. Nuts.

"If your foot is added to, why won't you have the pitch side camera to determine if there are germs in it?" reported the team Doctor.

"What's the game design?" to injure our opponents, did the Coach.

"Referee, referee, did you hear that?"

Every footballer steps on the football pitch with a game form. As the match goes on, these changes as team tactic change.

"What's your game plan?" asked the referee.

"To lose," repeated Mr. Nuts

Chapter 5

"A ENGLAND fan escaped from his seat to lead home early, the referee gave him a yellow card for time-wasting" read the Stewards.

He stumbled on his way out.

The referee asked him, "Why are you stumbling?"

"It's because you are stubborn," he reacted.

"They are at the traffic lights, please kidnap them and traffic them to the prison," declared the Coach.

"Who are they?" Mr. Nuts asked.

"The opponents!" he responded.

"This is blackmailing!" asserted Mr. Nuts.

"No it's black listing," responded the Coach.

"The opponents are too fat!" they can't fit in the car boot, read Mr. Nuts

"Chuck them in the Jail." Or else we will lose the match, expressed the Coach.

"Are you terrified of opposition?" claimed the referee.

"I fear their physic, too strong, too bad!" suggested the Coach.

"The European Cup is the toughest tournament in the field!" said the referee.

"Isn't it the European Cup the highest computer in the group" said Mr. Lion.

"Why are all the Buff players playing the FIFA World Cup competition?" added Mr. Little.

"Is the Cup mine?" ordered Mr. Little

'what drink?'

"The world Cup!" he suggested.

"try to earn it," declared the referee.

"I am freezing!" responded Mr. Lion.

"Let me take you out of the freezer," stated Mr. Little.

"The ball you kicked just flew past me!" is it a plane? Mr. Nuts asked.

"Let me review the ball!" asserted Mr. Little.

"No!-No you test the balls. Is it good to kick? Mr. Nuts said.

"My boots are dirty, I may need to obtain a boot cleaner," answered Mr. Lion.

''Why not engage me as a local shoplifter?" Said George.

"What's the colour of your boots?" it's green!

"Was it carried out from grass?" asked George.

"I made my boots from skin," responded Mr. Lion.

George replied, " did you say lattice?"

'No! Leather.'

'Lattice.'

"I was just checking because I have been searching for a leather boots to shoplift." answered George.

"Oh my God, I've just hired a thief," added Mr. Lion desperately.

"I need a fit to match my boots!" he continued.

'What suit?'

"Boiler suit because it's cold," suggested Mr. Lion.

"Your boots are white." Where they sent from heaven?" urged George.

"My feet can't fit my boots" declared Mr. Lion bewilderingly.

'Why?' It's because I made them for my hands, he replied.

"Where can I get football boots?" super drugs or BOOTS the chemist, George demanded.

"Your boots smell, are they from the toilet?" asked Mr. Nuts.

Chapter 6

"If the Knocks are too heavy, I will need to use flip-flops to play professional soccer," answered Mr. Lion.

'Referee, Referee, my boots are blind. I don't know in what direction the ball is heading.'

"I missed the football and kicked a stone but scored because the goalkeeper died in the dressing room," added Mr. Nuts.

"I used an abusive language and the referee sent me off with a medical label to get the Doctor," Mr. Nuts crushingly.

Perhaps the referee thought I needed to know a dirty language doctor for some treatment.

'I broke an opponent's leg and looked at a yellow card, two minutes later I breached the display and had shipped home for defecation.'

'I missed the football and error the air, they referee gave me a Passport to go to America.'

'Is the referee free?' let me check!

'Now the referee isn't available, he is busy fouling the air.'

'The ball hit the referee and the referee fouled the ball boy.'

"If you miss kick a player it's a yellow card but if the wind blows the flag poles it a new card," reported the referee

'If you give me your Green program, I will offer you a red card and I will ask you to leave the referee," asserted Mr. Nuts.

"When the referee used a foul language, I became injured," stated Mr. Little.

"Doctor, Doctor, there is something in the referee's mouth, isn't it food?" stated Mr. Lion.

"I have checked the polluted air, it's still in jet mode," declared Mr. Little amusingly.

'My teammate fouled me!'

'Why? He moved before the transfer window would open, added Mr. Lion.

"I will tell the Coach to resale him when the transfer window reopens because he isn't good enough," repeated Mr. Lion.

"My captain is a big cheat because he deflated the candidates before kicking off," declared Mr. Nuts.

I think the opponents must have been a spare wheel in a car.

"The team bus was once because it got stuck in traffic," asserted Mr. Lion.

"How far away is the bus driver?" asked Mr. Little.

"No, he is at turnstile asking for the players," responded Mr. Lion.

"Why was the team bus late?" Mr. Lion asked once more.

"It's because the bus was sick!" added Mr. Little.

"Did you take the club bus to the hospital for some treatment?" asked Mr. Nuts desperately.

"Yes, we took the team bus to the hospital, and they gave it an injection for it to get better," explained Mr. Little.

They were watching a match, and Mr. Lion spotted something.

"Is the referee tired?" he pleaded.

The assistant referee replied, "no I made him redundant"?

"What's that sound?"

"It was the referee begging for half time!"

"Why do our enemies love the referee?" asked Mr. Little.

I said, "is it because he is an injured player?"

"When will the referee be fit again?" I urged.

The assistant referee replied, "tomorrow a day after the match is over."

Chapter 7

Mr. Lion asked, "where is the referee now."

Our opponents acknowledged, "he is in our pocket!"

One player said, we demand an a wind break."

"What injury break?" asked Jake

"A ☐ pooping break," spoke Tom

Another shouted, "I am broken,"

Mr. Lion asked, "do you desire to see the Doctor?"

"No! I desire to see my toy," he told.

"Why aren't you running?"

"My tyres are flat," he replied.

I asked, are you a car, ?"

"It's my legs that are broken," announced Mr. Little.

"Should I fetch a mechanic?" asked Mr. Lion.

"Is the assistant referee playing football because I saw him?" he suggested.

What's your list "fired."

What's your surname "off!"

"Why are you always sent off, is it because you are a professional player?" Mr. Lion asked.

The actual name for Mr. sent off was sento, but his nickname was foul. He enjoyed fouling the opponents. Some of his offences were headbutting, injuring the knee cap, beating, knocking the referee and stamping on the assistant referee. Sent to always play on the blind side of the referee. He was huge, a giant in his own right.

The referee said, the only time I will address you off is to hell."

A player shouted, "referee, referee I will drop the assistant referee off if I caught him offside."

"Is the assistant referee is a cheat?" asked Mr. Lion.

"Why?" Because he drove the opponent's bus to the match, he did.

'What would I do if I caught Covid-19?' asked Mr. Nuts.

"I give it to the referee," asserted Mr. Little.

'Can a football cry?' Only when it's raining.

"Why is the referee running away from the football?" He fears he will be eaten by half time, told Mr. Nuts.

"When is the kids' world cup," urged Mr. Nuts.

"Next-door." the referee.

"Referee the assistant referee is hurt," declared Mr. Lion.

"By whom?" asked the referee.

"The football," replied Mr. Lion.

"Where's the assistant referee?" Mr. Little.

"He is hiding under a Duvet," replied Mr. Nuts.

'Is the assistant referee chatting?' No, he is cheating.

'Referee have you seen the Boy 'he is beating me!'

"We defeated a team 6-0, and they appealed in court," stated Mr. Lion.

The court refused to give a judgement because it was a matter for the referee to use his judgement.

'See, look, look the fans are singing!' Are they sinning?

"You aren't using the video properly," said broken Mr. Nuts.

"Why?" asked Mr. Little.

"It's because your vision is confused," he replied.

"Why is the man running on the television with a stick towards me?" Let me get up and run, did Mr. Little.

"Please call the police, the thief has jumped out of the television into my bedroom," announced Mr. Nuts.

"ENGLAND 0-5 Oldham. Why has the old sandwich won? Did the referee make the sandwich?" asked puzzled Mr. Nuts.

"Mr. Lion is a Buff, but he always scores after the final whistle is blown," asserted Mr. Little.

"When does an experienced referee blow the final whistle to end the game?" asked Mr. Lion.

"Isn't it the beginning of the trial?" asked Mr. Nuts.

The press had a brief interview with Mr. Nuts and all they spoke about was nuts.

The reporter suggested to the referee "is Mr. Nuts a mechanism."

The referee asked "why?"

"It's because he is a nutcracker," he replied.

Mr. Nuts told me the conversation was sweet.

Mr. Lion asked, "why, did you add sugar to it?"

He farted a dozen times suggested he ate some rotten eggs.

Mr. Nuts shouted at the cameraman "you aren't using the camera, is your vision confused?"

"Why is the cameraman at the centre of the pitch has it lost it bearings?" Mr. Little asked.

"Why is the camcorder at the gate?" demanded Mr. Nuts.

The Coach replied angrily, "I placed it there to catch the cheats on the pitch."

"Is the camera wearing a football kit?" it must be a player, Mr. Little wondered.

"Why is the camera treating an injured athlete on the pitch?" Mr. Lion replied, "I think it's the club doctor."

"The police camera captured a thief yesterday," replied Mr. Little.

'Where is he?'

"In my box" retorted Mr. Lion.

"Is the team bus a an athlete?" asked Mr. Nuts.

"Why?" Mr. Little asked.

Mr. Nuts replied, "it's because it's part of the club."

"They caught Mr. Nuts yesterday," added Mr. Lion.

"Where?" called for his friend.

"In a nutshell," Mr. Lion replied.

"The team bus is moving fast, and soon it will be the coach," responded Mr. Lion.

"Why are the professionals more famous than the team bus?" claimed the referee seemingly.

Mr. Lion replied, "it's because I always park it in the corner."

"Why does the team bus make less money than the players?" suggested Mr. Nuts.

Mr. Lion replied, " it's because the team bus is a beggar."

"I saw the team bus running?" said the referee.

"Perhaps he is a player," the assistant referee replied.

The camera liked the assistant referee, so he picked him up and gave him a lift in his car.

Someone told me that the point side camera has failed.

So, I called for 'why?'

The person replied, 'it didn't pass it exams.

Later that evening, I read in the newspapers that the angle side camera can't cover the pitch.

So, I sought 'why?'

The journalist replied, 'it's because it is not a blanket.'

Is the team bus the boss?

'Why ask?' it's because I thought he was the Coach.

"Why does the team bus get wheels?" inquired Mr. Nuts.

"It's because it enjoys snowboarding," replied Mr. Lion.

The player with the most moved is Ronaldo, is he going in the footballing transfer window?

"Where are you going during the footballing transfer window?" asked Mr. Lion.

"Are you moving to a new house?" the referee asked.

"Is Mr. Lion a mess?" demanded Mr. Little.

"Why did you ask?" pleaded Mr. Nuts with an intense gaze.

"It's because he resembles Ronaldo," he replied.

"Why did Mr. Lion escape it prison and stained my pyjamas?" begged Mr. Nuts.

"That's because he is a colour," responded Mr. Little.

"Why is my pyjamas a chameleon?" asked Mr. Little.

'No idea'

"It's because it has changed colour since Mr. Lion escaped it prison," asserted Mr. Little.

Mr. Lion forgot to shut it mouth,

It kept running and running into my towel.

"My toothbrush is yellow could I have made it from Mr. Lion's pyjamas? " Asked Mr. Little.

"Why is Mr. Lion fading?" asked Mr. Nuts.

"Perhaps he is a sick colour," suggested Mr. Little.

When I washed my pyjamas I soon found out it was running a race.

When I investigated further, it was racist against my pet.

The Suarez artwork is missing, perhaps it has called on the wood burner.

I made some art with Mr. Lion, but a rat ate it.

"When will Mr. Lion return my portrait?" urged Mr. Little.

"When it has called on the wood oven," replied Mr. Nuts with tears in his eyes.

"Is Mr. Lion blind?" demanded the referee.

"It is because he is a colour that knows no boundaries," he countered.

"Is Mr. Lion the drive of the school bus?" pleaded Mr. Little.

"No idea," declared the referee.

"It's because he has just changed into the wheels of the bus," he retorted.

"Mr. Lion is yelling," answered the referee.

'Why?'

"It's because he's just turned nuts after moving to the wrong club," said Mr. Little.

Mr. Lion is a star on the football pitch, is he the floodlights?

"Mr. Lion is bright, has he just arrived at the supermarket to get more colours," said the referee

"Who is the golden boots winner, perhaps it's the referee," said Mr. Nuts.

Chapter 8

Mr. Lion smelled a foul air with disgust.

"Lioness have you farted? Hah! It's the tricky smell that had been coming a while ago from your pants," whined Lioness. Mr. Lion glanced at the door to ensure no one heard him "it most be the leftover sweat on my boots."

Yak you had stunk of sweat months ago,"

"Its show's how prepared I am for the tournament," address Mr. Lion.

"I will have lied hadn't I told you so." Said Lady Lioness.

'Thank you!' Mr. Lion approached with a hug.

Lioness escaped his gesture, leaving a piece of herself in the tin air between them.

'Don't touch me, you stink like you've been swimming in a pile of shit yak.'

"Will you say that when I bring the trophy □ home," asserted Mr. Lion.

"Please have a bath," said Lioness.

'I most leave at once.'

"We have been joking about poop for a long time, but I never thought my brother will be the poop collector," told her sister Lioness.

He passed the sparking few drenched grass on a crisp cold December evening in the English countryside. There stood a doghouse at the front porch of the peak thatched roof of his coach house.

The fresh roses hadn't smelt foul for a couple of months until when Mr. Lion came along. Even the flies couldn't bare the lingering odour.

Mr. Lion took St Michael's Drive, down into Clarendon mew. As soon as he approached Woodcote Road, he bounced into Mr. Little and Mr. Nuts his classmates. He tried to bend the other way into Stanley Park Avenue. When he heard his phone ran.

"I saw your branching of Stanley Park Avenue, are you off to report at the dump□□"

"Not at all, I am in a rush,

Before he knew it, they've caught up with him. 'Hey dumpster, are you in trouble again?' Mr. Nuts quizzed.

'Let's do him a favour take him to the car wash for some sparkling quick jet wash!' Mr.

Little. Are you new? The news is that you stink.

Mr. Nuts trouser became entangled with a mob and the elasticized band reversed him to the nod of the wood. He hit the tree and bounced off it with a great gash across his forehead dropping back down on the ground the entire string of events left him mock of sweat.

At a glance everything was normal.

Mr. Little took a mobile phone to capture the sequence of affairs whilst Mr. Lion glanced around to see if others have experienced what he'd witnessed.

Mr. Lion pressed his hands against Mr. Nuts chest to observe his heart beat, With one hand on his paws to investigate his blood flow, but there wasn't any sign of life. Had Mr. Nuts shit himself to death? Thought Mr. Lion.

Mr. Little began murmuring,

Mr. Nuts lips paced in a while, his first words were a patched work of low-pitched sentences.

"Sorry, Mr. Lion."

"I didn't mean to hurt you, by the way, your stinky boots smell better than me," Mr. Nuts explained.

A pleasing wide smile Rose from Mr. Lion's cheeks, it's seems as if they had restored his reputation in a gratifying fashion. There was a punch in the air, with his fist bouncing off his chest. The joy he felt was plain to see. Now there was parity. There was nothing Mr. Nuts would say about him without accusing him of the same. Mr. Nuts was a friend but the biggest bully in their year group. He was fat and ugly, but never wished for a word that he resembled a monster.

Mr. Nuts grew up in a single-parent household and raised by his grandma until she passed away. He was lucky enough to get a scholarship to a top-notch prep school. With all the worst experiences in life, Mr. Nuts remarkable achievement made me burst with joy when I had his story.

His mother was a cleaner in a hospital. At age five Mr. Nuts was tasked with the responsibility of tidying the house, caring for his sick Grandma and taking his stepbrothers and sister to school. Despite these, Mr. Nuts achieved the best grades in his year group. One will say he was a remarkable young man.

There was a slight rush of blood and a rising in temperature on Mr. Nuts, otherwise he was fine with a few gusts of shameful touch on his face. As Mr. Little investigated the event, she stumbled and fell on a fresh dog poo.

Ha! Ha!! Ha!!! Noise' Mr. Nuts couldn't bare but laugh.

While Mr. Lion's amusement coursed rapid heartbeat and shortness of breath. Although he was surprised at the speed of events, it delighted him to see them in the same predicaments, now that the three of them were dirty and stunk.

Mr. Lion shouted with laughter 'Mr stinker.'

Mr. Nuts screamed, "chief dumpster, you will dump any team in any tournament, its no wonder you smell of sweat."

Then replied Mr. Little, "I am the chair of the stench,"

Mr. Nuts Asked "when did you smell?"

Mr. Lion replied, "I have always smelled of sweet perfumes."

88

"Next week, I shall take my position in the sewer," said Mr. Little.

"You have already done so," acknowledged Mr. Nuts.

"Who smells the most," suggested Mr. Little

"Me." inquired Mr. Little.

"That's because I smell like a millionaire." suggested Mr. Lion the dumpster.

"I think we should have a soccer tournament" said Mr. Nuts.

Moments later Mr. Nuts fainted. Could this be it Mr. Nuts ultimate moment's with us? Panicked Mr. Lion.

'What should we do?'

'What should we do?'

Nothing like this had never occurred in their lives. They stood there watching each other for a good ten minutes. The sun was scorching. There was a slight breeze from the North West. All the children's hospitals were on the other side of town. Without money, they were hopeless. Surely, no institution will hold them in.

"When a man who was a Doctor was passing by and went to their aid."

He suggested the request for the ambulance to pick up Mr. Nuts to hospital. The ambulance arrived two minutes late, and all of them joined the paramedic to the nearest emergency room.

Upon arrival other Doctors were waiting at the door perhaps to tell sick patients don't come here or else we will cure you.

Five hours later Mr. Nuts was discharged from concussion.

What a miracle to recover the same day, perhaps it was his glut that kept him alive.

On their way home Mr. Lion questioned him further, but he was uncompromising.

Mr. Lion confessed "my actions were deliberate, I work in a football club and I wonder if my manager would guarantee a soccer tournament?"

Mr. Lion "don't worry, I will let you know by noon tomorrow."

They settled and went their separate ways.

At noon the next day Mr. Lion brought them great news the club has granted to fund the football contest.

"Great, it's wonderful news" replied Mr. Nuts.

"See you there," Mr. Little.

"I shall be ready for you," Mr. Lion.

"You won't win unless you prevent" Mr. Nuts.

"You forget I already play football" said Mr. Lion

“so do I!” Mr. Nuts --_-----.

Mr. Little spoke belatedly, “You can't deceive the clock and besides, I am the chair of the game.” You can't knock me off my porch. Too bad for you!

“You talk as if we’re the only competitors!” Mr. Lion briefed the stand.

“Well I have had a head start with an ancient practice” retorted Mr. Nuts.

“You don’t know what the vacation are up to,” Mr. Lion.

“ Speak for yourself and not others!” suggested Mr. Little.

“I can’t stay to prove my skills,” lamented Mr. Nuts.

“So what?” you can’t expect to knock your brain off the tree again □□□□□□□□. Mr. Lion replied.

"This time a million people will laugh at you," said Mr. Little.

"Why?" asked Mr. Nuts.

"Because you are a fool," said Mr. Lion.

"Mr. Lion, you are no competition for me, the only person I am worried about is Mr. Little," said Mr. Nuts.

"Why Mr. Little?"

"Its because he got skills to knock himself into a skillful tournament," Mr. Nuts replied.

"Why again" Mr. Lion quizzed.

" Its takes guts to head into a tournament unprepared."

' That doesn't complete the puzzle' I am intrigued.

" Keep your intrigue to yourself'

"No need to vex over a competition that only kids care about!" suggested Mr. Little.

" Really, particularly kids will be there," Mr. Lion.

"Look I have just passed away from my birthday!" replied Mr. Lion.

"Surely you don't want to be born on that date any more" as you don't wish to remember it any longer. Mr. Little said.

"No, I went away with the ☐ cake and left them to celebrate the crumbs," added Mr. Lion.

"I hate my birthday!" he continued.

Mr. Little asked, "Why?"

"Because I've been fighting my month of creation!" repeated Mr. Lion.

"you must like something about your maternal day?" if not give it to me, I shall make it world fool's day, Mr. Nuts suggested.

"Isn't it first of April?" said Mr. Little.

"That's the date all the Lions were born!" said Mr. Nuts.

"What's wrong with birth date?" Mr. Nuts.

"Are you suggesting I am a Lion?" Mr. Lion asked.

"A minute ago you hated your birthday, and now you want to claim a Lions birth why Mr. Lion?" asked Mr. Nuts.

"It's my birthday alright!" said Mr. Lion.

"I am going to clean myself up then go and celebrate what leftover from my after tounament party." Said Mr. Lion.

The tournament began England breezed passed the group stage.

In the quarter finals England flow passed it opponent

No team matched England's skills.

At the end of the tournament, the trophy was won.

Chapter 9

"I must return to my sister's house for my after tounament celebrations," declared Mr. Lion.

"What a party!" replied Mr. Little.

"I am coming with you to enjoy myself," stated Mr. Nuts.

"Do you want to end joy?" you joy killer! Asked Mr. Lion.

"No, not at all, I will be there to make Joy because it's your occasion," repeated Mr. Nuts.

"What's that English?" are you telling me you will make Joy because it's my mechanical day?" Mr. Lion.

"Non sense, I will Merry because it's a special occasion," suggested Mr. Nuts.

"Mr. Nuts are you serious, you've called my after tournament party a mechanical day, and now you are saying you will be merry on my maternal day?" asserted Mr. Lion.

"Eat grass you aren't having any of my Stew," he continued.

"Please hold me there, if we make now I will leave early," added Mr. Nuts.

"There's a boy called Ali, Ali, take him to a mental hospital he isn't well," responded Mr. Lion.

"If you miss this opportunity to cure him, he will run mad," announced Mr. Lion.

"Please let go!" begged Mr. Nuts.

"OK I will take you there if you don't eat my food," Mr. Lion.

"OK, ok I promise."

They walked through the faded light into a dark corridor leading into an old disused railway line.

There stood some boys shivering from the cold chilly wind. They could see smoke rising in a distance. Perhaps it's a steam train arriving from Birmingham.

One child shouted from a distance the train is coming while at the same time racing to catch it.

Is he Black because he could be racist?

Mr. Lion said, " never mind, we aren't catching the line."

Mr. Nuts responded, what are we here for? Catching flies?"

"No, my sister's house is at the opposite end of the railway station," suggested Mr. Lion.

"How far?"

"A quick stroll from here," stated Mr. Lion.

"But I can only smell toxic fumes and no stew. Is it perhaps the party is over?" answered Mr. Nuts.

"My friend, you aren't going there for my drink, the more you eat, the more dirty farts comes from you," added Mr. Lion.

'OK!'

"When we get there, if they give you any cook to eat pass it over and say you're fed up," reported Mr. Lion.

"Why?"

"I will tell you tomorrow after I have eaten the meal," suggested Mr. Lion.

"I wish you good luck, Mr. Nuts, but honestly, there isn't a chance for you." You should go home and eat grasshoppers," mocked Mr. Lion.

"Why the gesture?" asked Mr. Nuts.

Mr. Lion's smile turned into the smell of something. I suppose food.

He eventually replied, "it's not laugh it's later my friend I am leaving you here, now is the time to path company."

"Yak, too bad I will follow you wherever you go," Mr. Nuts.

"I lost you I must take you to the police station," declared Mr. Lion.

"What for?" inquired Mr. Nuts.

"So you can find your Web address," asserted Mr. Lion.

"Non sense don't be silly we are there already," declared Mr. Nuts.

"OK beef eater, you will only drink water and nothing else you hear me!" repeated Mr. Lion.

"What's that grin?" urged Mr. Lion.

"What's that smell?" demanded Mr. Nuts.

Mr. Lion slapped his head and maintained be quiet.

Lioness glanced at Mr. Nuts have you dined?"

Mr. Nuts nodded yes with a gentle laugh.

"What's the beam about "that's because you claimed I should eat ten plates," suggested Mr. Nuts.

"Nope, I said eaten, not feed ten!" replied Lioness.

"Do you want a non-alcoholic beer?" asked Lioness.

"Did you ask I need non-catholic pair?" suggested Mr. Nuts.

"Am I wasting my life here?" asked Lioness.

"OK dishes are dirty I better wash them," said Lioness.

"Are the debt on the dish huge?" urged Mr. Nuts.

Em "see you later" Lioness left to freshen up the plates.

Mr. Lion need to fresh up before talking to me this second round.

"Great luck" said Lioness.

"I must fetch a suitable joined to lock him up, so he stops bothering me about food," repeated Mr. Nuts.

"I am going to tell Mr. Lion its lockdown time. You can't ask me for meat any longer. It's Covid-19 time everyone is sealed up in doors period," murmured Mr. Nuts.

"I always meltdown when I catch him but have got no liquid to show for it," he continued.

Josh spoke, "so you got to the side."

"Yes, I got to the tea dinner," Mr. Nuts replied.

"Are you drunk?" suggested Josh.

"Nope, are you dumb?" begged Mr. Nuts.

"Well, I most leave you now, another time," said Josh.

"OK" Mr. Nuts.

Mr. Nuts took a brief glance and saw Mr. Lion.

The Hunter was becoming the hunted.

Mr. Lion said, " meet me there!"

Mr. Nuts replied, " mate I am in!"

"Remember, it's my after tournament party all the food belongs to me," answered Mr. Lion.

"Are you a spider?" asked Mr. Nuts.

"Please mind your language!" said Mr. Lion.

He went for his food; therefore he felt to be a fool. He told Mr. Nuts the wheat should fill his plate and his eyes were on him. Furthermore, he should bring the food directly to him.

Mr. Nuts took the first one and ate it. No sooner he'd done, so he received a slap on his head. Mr. Nuts promised him a refreshment of Fanta, so he kept his promise.

Mr. Lion, your belly is shining. If you consume the cherry aid Fanta, you may die of food disease.

"I've heard it all before, it all nonsense,"

" Any more leftovers?" asked Mr. Nuts.

Mr. Lion replied, "When have you become a beggar?"

Mr. Lion continued, 'I am not in a fit present to eat.'

'I know you are in the farting state now.'
You've won the football tournament.

"Is your belly drunk?"

"I drew my belly to the toilet, that's where I belong tonight!" stated Mr. Lion.

"It's a shame you tried to be a spider," repeated Mr. Nuts.

"Let me entertain you," answered Mr. Lion.

"With what?" asked Mr. Little.

"With a sock ball," replied Mr. Lion.

There comes the final whistle, must be the end of the match.

Someone kind appreciated your reviews.

You can leave reviews on AMAZON

Thanks for your support.

You can follow my Facebook page @

author Bry Johnson Free Kids books and

videos,

Or

Saferlane parents & kids fun activities

Printed in Great Britain
by Amazon